HH

The Great Pants Robbery

'The Great Pants Robbery'
An original concept by Heather Pindar
© Heather Pindar

Illustrated by Serena Lombardo

Published by MAVERICK ARTS PUBLISHING LTD

Studio 3A, City Business Centre, 6 Brighton Road,

Horsham, West Sussex, RH13 5BB

© Maverick Arts Publishing Limited March 2019

+44 (0)1403 256941

A CIP catalogue record for this book is available at the British Library.

ISBN 978-1-84886-436-8

Maverick
publishing
www.maverickbooks.co.uk

White

This book is rated as: White Band (Guided Reading)

The Great Pants Robbery

By **Heather Pindar**

Illustrated by
Serena Lombardo

Chapter 1

It was a normal Saturday afternoon in Little Snorington - sensible, quiet and maybe a teensy bit boring. Most people were at home doing chores, or out shopping. The only sound was the gentle putt-putting of lawnmowers.

But then there was a sudden, ear-splitting shriek. The mowers stopped putt-putting.

Mrs Gubbins rushed out of her gate. "Call Sergeant Bodgit," she gasped. "They've taken my underwear! All of it! There's not a single pair of pants left on my washing line!"

Grandma Lil hurried outside. Her dog Sniffy followed close behind.

Lil invited Mrs Gubbins indoors and gave her a cup of strong, sweet tea.

"What's happening, Gran?" asked Lil's granddaughter, Julia.

"There's a pants robber on the loose," said Grandma Lil. "Poor Mrs Gubbins, she's been left with only the pants she's wearing! Go and tell Sergeant Bodgit, Julia."

"OK, Gran, I know where he'll be!" said Julia. She raced up the street, past the police station, and through a little gate.

She was right! There was Bodgit on his allotment, weeding his lettuces. Julia told him about Mrs Gubbins' pants being stolen.

"Alright," said Bodgit wearily. "I'll look into it. But first I need to feed my goats. They're special Ibex Mountain Goats* you know."

*Ibex Mountain Goats are amazing climbers. They are famous for climbing up a very high wall in Italy. The hooves of these goats are split into two toes. Each toe is soft in the middle so it can grip onto tiny bits of rock.

In the next few days, there was a lot of muttering in Little Snorington. Almost all of that muttering was about Sergeant Bodgit. Lots of people were cross that he hadn't managed to track down the pants robber.

But soon things got worse! All over town, pants began to disappear. At the police station, there were lots of reports of empty washing lines and chilly bottoms.

Chapter 2

Grandma Lil was worried. She owned a collection of very special pants - her trapeze pants. They were beautifully coloured, with sequins and a cosy woollen lining. When Lil put them on, she remembered her circus days. She felt again the rush of air as she flew across the Big Top, and she heard the audience 'aah-ing' and 'ooh-ing' below.

But the time came when Lil had run out of clean trapeze pants. There was no choice – she would have to wash them, and run the risk that the pants robber might strike.

She washed her pants as usual, by hand. She looked at the labels. DO NOT TUMBLE DRY. DON'T JUST POP ON THE RADIATOR INSTEAD.

Lil sighed. "They have to go on the washing line to dry," she told Sniffy. "I'm giving you a very important job. Watch these pants and guard them with your life!"

"Rrrrr. Raff, raff!" barked Sniffy enthusiastically.

"Good dog," said Grandma Lil. "I'm going shopping. I'll be back soon."

Sniffy settled down under the washing line.

He kept his eyes, ears, nose and whiskers alert.

If the pants robber came, Sniffy would be ready.

At first, everything was quiet. The pants
steamed slightly in the warm air. Then Sniffy
looked up sharply. The washing line was shaking.

Sniffy jumped up. What was that smell?
It couldn't be...

...GOAT! A robber goat standing on the fence and nibbling at the washing line.

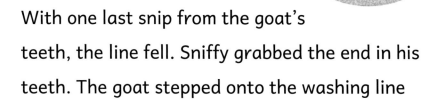

"*Grrr!* Gerrroff. Raff, raff, raff!" barked Sniffy angrily.

With one last snip from the goat's teeth, the line fell. Sniffy grabbed the end in his teeth. The goat stepped onto the washing line pole and nibbled swiftly through the other end of the line. Sniffy pulled. The robber goat pulled. They were having a tug of war with Grandma Lil's precious trapeze pants!

Sniffy growled fiercely. The robber goat opened her mouth slightly and...

...the washing line fell to the ground.

Sniffy flew backwards into the street.

"Raff! Raff!" he yapped excitedly. He raced along the pavement, towing the line of trapeze pants. Passers-by stared. Finally the line got tangled around the bus shelter and Sniffy came to a sudden stop.

"Sniffy! It was Sniffy all along!" shouted Mrs Gubbins. "We all saw you steal those pants. We're taking you to Sergeant Bodgit."

Chapter 3

"Sniffy's at the police station!" Grandma Lil told Julia worriedly.

"I heard, Gran," said Julia. "But I've got a plan to prove Sniffy isn't the pants robber."

"Sniffy's a bit cheeky sometimes, but he's no thief," agreed Lil.

"It's lucky Sniffy kept your trapeze pants safe," said Julia. "You're going to need them."

Chapter 4

An hour or two later, Julia's plan was ready.
Lots of people had lent her pairs of pants,
and she had pegged them on to Grandma Lil's
trapeze line. Everything was set for Grandma Lil
to finish the job.

"I don't know how I let you talk me into this,
Julia," said Lil.

"Which trapeze pants did you decide to wear,
Gran?" asked Julia.

"The purple ones," chuckled Lil. "They're my luckiest pants. And I'll need plenty of luck for this job."

Lil took the line of pants from Julia, and climbed up the first lamppost. She knotted the trapeze line around the top of the lamppost. Then Lil waved to Julia, grabbed the rope firmly and swung towards the second lamppost.

"Wahooo! I haven't lost my touch!" yelled Lil. She carried on down the road, swinging from lamppost to lamppost and tying up the line as she went. Soon there was a long line of fluttering pants all the way to the police station.

"Go Gran! You're amazing!" said Julia.

"Thank you, dear!" said Lil. "Now all we have to do is wait. The real robber can spot these pants from miles away."

It was well past teatime when Julia noticed someone was climbing up to reach the pants.

"Look, Gran! It's the **PANTS ROBBER**... and she's a **GOAT!**"

"Hmm. Looks like she finds pants very **TASTY** indeed. She's starting to eat the lot!" said Gran.

"Sergeant Bodgit! Emergency!" yelled Julia.

Bodgit strolled out of the police station.

"What's the fuss about?" said Sergeant Bodgit. "I'm busy telling off your thieving Sniffy."

"Nonsense, Bodgit!" said Lil. "There's the real pants robber!"

"Don't be silly," Bodgit scoffed. "Goats can't climb things. Who put Sancha up there?"

"Sancha! So the pants robber is your goat," said Julia. "And yes, they can! Aren't Ibex Mountain

Goats the best climbers?"

Bodgit looked nervous.

"Sniffy is innocent, let him go!" Julia said firmly.

"Not so fast," said Bodgit. "Sancha is eating the pants, I'll give you that. But someone made her do it. My Sancha was led astray by Sniffy. Sniffy is the true criminal mastermind in this case."

Chapter 5

"Quiet everyone! Silence in court!" Judge Penelope Stern waited for some newcomers to find seats at the back of the room.

"We have heard how Sniffy and Sancha have both been caught in the act of **PANTS STEALING**. Has anyone else got anything to say that might help us, err, get to the *bottom* of this case?"

"We do!" yelled a group of people at the back.

"They came, Gran!" whispered Julia delightedly.

"Alright," said Judge Stern. "What do you want to tell the court?"

A tall, bearded man stepped forward. He began reading. "June 5th, 3.10 p.m: pants stolen from Mrs Gubbin's washing line. June 5th, 3.10 p.m: Sniffy seen chewing tyres on Mr. Anderson's car."

"June 12th, 11.10 a.m: pants stolen from Mr

Adam Dimpleby. June 12th, 11.10 a.m: Sniffy chasing the number 7 bus to Upper Snorington."

"June 14th, 2pm: pants stolen from Sheeplick Lane. June 14th, 2pm: Sniffy caught digging holes in..."

"Thank you!" interrupted Judge Stern. "We get the picture. Clearly Sniffy is a very naughty dog indeed. But he is not the **PANTS ROBBER** – not unless he can be in two places at one time. Sniffy is free to go."

There was a loud cheer from the back. Sniffy scurried across the room and leapt into Julia's arms.

"I'm sorry to say that Sancha is a danger to pants everywhere. She will need to stay in custody."

"Custardy?" said Bodgit. "Sancha doesn't even like custard!"

"No, no, Bodgit," said Judge Stern. "Custody. In jail. Locked up!"

"Oh, custody. Why didn't you say so?" said Bodgit. "My Sancha won't need custody.

She can come with me."

"Come with you where, Bodgit?" asked Judge Stern.

"To the farm. I've bought a farm far up in the hills for all my goats. I'm retiring from being a police officer."

"Aha!" said Judge Stern, "If Sancha is going to live far away from washing lines and other people's pants, she won't be tempted to steal them. Sancha is free to go."

"Thanks, Judge!" said Bodgit.

Someone clapped him on the back. "Good luck, Bodgit!"

"Gran," said Julia, as they left the courtroom. "Please can you give me some trapeze lessons?"

"Oh yes, dear!" said Lil. "But first we must go shopping. You'll need some warm trapeze pants – you wouldn't believe how chilly it gets high up on a trapeze."

The people of Little Snorington returned happily to their sensible and quiet lives. But they never forgot the Great Pants Robbery. And once a year, as a special treat, they send a parcel of pants to Sancha.

The End

Book Bands for Guided Reading

Pink

Red

Yellow

Blue

Green

Orange

Turquoise

Purple

Gold

White

The Institute of Education book banding system is a scale of colours that reflects the various levels of reading difficulty. The bands are assigned by taking into account the content, the language style, the layout and phonics. Word, phrase and sentence level work is also taken into consideration.

Maverick Early Readers are a bright, attractive range of books covering the pink to white bands. All of these books have been book banded for guided reading to the industry standard and edited by a leading educational consultant.

To view the whole Maverick Readers scheme, visit our website at www.maverickearlyreaders.com

Or scan the QR code above to view our scheme instantly!